3 DAYS WITH A COWBOY

LACY WILLIAMS

For Mr. Bingley. My walking partner, bringer-of-smiles, and the best dog a girl could ever ask for. I miss you.

With thanks to Randy Ingermanson for help making Jake more authentic.

CHAPTER 1

*E*ffect: Red dust rose in clouds over the entrance to his property.

Cause: Someone was coming up the drive.

Jake Sutton straightened from beneath the hood of the farm truck that was as old as he was and pulled off his gloves, stuffing the dusty leather into his back pocket.

He knocked back his Stetson with one knuckle as he watched the compact hybrid rattle over the rutted red dirt drive. Bright October sunlight glared off the windshield. A car like that was not made for the farm track.

Who in the world was that?

He'd lived in Redbud Trails his whole life, minus the ten years he'd spent at university. Been back for the last five. There were five hundred eighty-three families in Redbud Trails, and he didn't know a single one with a hybrid car. It wasn't practical on the bumpy farm roads around here.

The drive ran alongside the house and gave easy

access to both the front and back doors. The red car stopped in the shade of the two-story farmhouse toward the back—the driver must have seen Jake by the barn. He walked over to say hello, because his mom had preached good manners throughout his entire childhood. The engine shut off.

When the driver stepped out, Jake felt like he'd had his breath knocked out of him.

Stevie Flower.

Her raven black hair was cut in a trendy chin-length style and her eyes—eyes he knew to be a shade of near-transparent blue—were hidden behind sunglasses that he supposed were stylish but were so big they dwarfed her elfin features.

The probability of a visit from Stevie Flower was so close to zero it was immeasurable.

And yet here she was.

Shouldn't she be in Nashville, recording a new album or planning a tour or something?

"Hey," he said when the silence—and her stare—unnerved him.

"Hi, Jake."

She remembered his name?

Her nose wrinkled, and one corner of her mouth ticked slightly upward. "It hasn't been that long since high school."

Not long enough.

Had he spoken his first thought aloud? He couldn't control the shock that was tying up his tongue and causing the back of his neck to itch. At least the morning breeze cut beneath the brim of his Stetson and cooled him off a bit.

Stevie was a country music artist, one of the hottest new voices getting airtime, though he knew she'd gone to Nashville over a decade ago to try and make a career for herself.

He took in her trendy clothes, those stylish sunglasses. The car. Her presence still didn't compute. "How'd you find me out here?"

He'd bought this place five years ago, but when he'd been a kid, his family had lived in town.

Her face turned slightly to one side ,and the muscles in her cheek bunched and released. He was no good at reading facial expressions. Was she embarrassed? Chagrined about what she was about to say? "I might've done a little bit of Facebook stalking."

He felt his mouth unhinge. Each inhale and exhale puffed through his open lips. But he couldn't manage to close it. *Stevie* had been looking *him* up? Why?

"I didn't know you'd be here today though," she said.

"Fall break." The long weekend away from his job as a physics professor was supposed to be relaxing. But while his colleagues would be working on making the next big breakthrough in their fields, he would be catching up on the farm work that had been piling up over these past weeks.

More awkward silence, this time so quiet that he could hear the far off leaves of the peach orchard rattling in the breeze. Then Stevie's lips twisted, and her chin lifted as she turned her face toward the barn.

He pushed away the starstruck thoughts and really *looked* at the woman.

And he finally registered the fine lines around her mouth and the tense set of her shoulders. She hadn't taken off her sunglasses—was she hiding behind them?

He took a step toward her. "Are you in trouble?"

FOR ONE VAIN MOMENT, Stevie Flower was glad she'd stopped at a gas station in Weatherford and re-applied her makeup.

She was used to admiration from her fans and hangers-on, but the Jake she'd known back in high school hadn't been one to pander. It made his admiration and embarrassment humbling.

Although...the man in front of her bore little resemblance to the Jake she remembered.

He'd filled out the lanky frame he'd had in school. He was still tall, probably six-six in his boots, but his shoulders were broad and sturdy. He wore stylish, black-rimmed glasses beneath his Stetson. Back then, he'd always had his nose stuck in an advanced textbook.

She'd come expecting a scientist. She'd gotten a cowboy.

She was distracted by the way his chest filled out his T-shirt beneath the flannel shirt he wore unbuttoned. The T-shirt bore a scientific notation of some kind instead of a logo. $dT/dt = -k(T-Ts)$. Beneath the equation was simply the word "cool."

After the stillness of being in the car for the last ten

hours, the brisk breeze made her eyes sting with tears. It smelled fresh and earthy, not like the stale scents of fast food that clung to her.

The barn behind him had been decorated to look like a spooky face with two huge yellow eyes tacked to the wall above the wide-open door and fangs hanging down from the crossbeam just above the threshold. In the distance, gold and orange leaves on the trees announced that fall was here.

She'd felt a strange, empty aching in her chest the moment she'd turned off the highway and onto the gravel road that ran in front of Jake's property. Maybe it was a miracle she could feel anything at all.

Her thoughts swirled an allegro, jumping from one thing to the next. If she allowed too much of a pause, they would start to drift to...

Grief slashed inside, throwing her internal refrain into discord, and she grabbed onto the last thing he'd asked her. *Are you in trouble?*

He was patient, still waiting for her to collect herself, although her long pause bordered on rudeness.

"I need a place to stay for a couple of days," she said.

His brows rose slightly, the only visible reaction he gave. "All right. I've got a spare bedroom."

Relief sang through her, making her eyes sting again. She breathed in deeply through her nose, trying to stem the tide. Her smile felt wobbly when it came. "This is crazy."

Maybe *she* was crazy, to have come here like this. But

the hope that Jake would be able to help her remained lodged just beneath the knot in her throat.

He took a step nearer, his boot crunching in the gravel drive. "I don't know about crazy, but I'm always willing to help out a friend in need."

Friend. How long had it been since she'd had a real one? She had hangers-on and fans and her *business manager*, Zack, but she'd been burned in Nashville enough times—including once by her supposed best friend—that she kept important things close to the vest. In her pocket, her phone dinged a new text message.

Zack again. She owed her manager a call, but not now.

Before her shifting emotions could circle back to tears, she ducked her head into the still-open drivers' side door and reached across the console for her duffel bag. She hadn't really taken time to pack last night. She'd thrown a few things into the duffel and gotten in her car.

Then she'd driven all night.

She'd started without a real destination in mind, just known she had to get out. Out of her sterile apartment. Out of Nashville.

Maybe even out of the music industry.

About two hours into her westward journey, she'd remembered Jake. Remembered what he'd gone through back in high school. And that kernel of hope had taken root in her chest.

"Do you mind if I go in and freshen up a little? I drove all night."

His eyebrows twitched again. He was pretty good at

cloaking his expressions, but not as good as the folks she was used to. "Sure. Bedroom's on the second floor, third door on the right. Bathroom's right next to it." He jerked his thumb over his shoulder. "I've got a load of pumpkins to attend to, but I'll be in at lunchtime."

Pumpkins?

She closed the car door and turned toward the house. It was a two-story farmhouse, clean and neat, just like the barnyard. The house faced the road, even though it was a ways down the drive. If she had to guess, that meant this long porch and back door must lead into the kitchen.

She went up the steps and through the door, her energy flagging. Maybe she would lie down for a bit.

Maybe she was finally tired enough to be able to sleep without thinking about...

It was cool and dim in the kitchen, light streaming in from a window above the sink. She pushed her sunglasses back on her head, thankful Jake was still outside and wouldn't see her red-streaked eyes. The floor creaked underfoot, a sound she equated with her childhood and the farmhouse her parents had owned. Smells of floury biscuits and coffee had her stomach rumbling. She hadn't stopped since the middle of the night.

Through a large arch, she could see a dining area off to one side and a hallway with a set of stairs running parallel to it. A TV played from somewhere further inside.

It didn't look like a bachelor's place. There were kitchen towels—matching ones—folded neatly on the counter. There was no detritus from the breakfast meal on the nook table. The dishwasher hummed and swished beneath the counter. A set of decorative pumpkins rested along one counter.

Sudden unease rippled through her. She'd snooped online but Jake's relationship status had read "single." She hadn't thought to look at his left hand—was he married?

And then her stomach pinched as she took in the childish artwork hanging on the refrigerator.

Movement from the hall brought her head around, and blood rushed to her temples, sending pulsing pain through her skull.

A little sprite in jeans and pink cowgirl boots stood in the archway, a small, white Stetson clutched against her belly.

"Who're you?" the girl asked.

STEVIE FLOWER.

Stevie was in his house.

Jake returned to the farm truck parked next to the barn and the one-thousand eight hundred thirty-three pumpkins he needed to bring up from the back field.

Forget being starstruck. He'd seen the way her lips had trembled. Her attention had spun every which way. It had taken her way too long to get into the conversation he'd started.

She hadn't admitted outright to being in trouble, but something was wrong. And she'd come to him.

He didn't get it. They hadn't spoken since *that day* in

high school. Memories of those fateful few minutes were branded in his brain, a warning he'd heeded every time he'd been tempted to ask a woman out.

He gripped the cap on the oil tank and tightened it. At least he'd finished changing the old truck's oil before she got here. Wouldn't have the brain power for even that job now.

He was two years her junior. During his sophomore year, he'd already been taking Physics 201 through concurrent enrollment at the university in Weatherford. His high school physics teacher had asked him to tutor her.

He'd had a disproportionately large crush on her. In his defense, so had every other guy at their high school. Who wouldn't? She'd been beautiful even back then, and musical. She'd played the lead in the school play in both her junior and senior years. But when he'd been one-on-one with her, studying in the library, she'd been sweeter than he could have imagined.

And then he'd let himself do something stupid.

Was allowing her to stay with him another stupid mistake? He was comfortable enough with himself to admit he didn't always understand others' social cues. More accurately—he spent more time focusing on his work than worrying about what the people around him were feeling.

But right about now, he wished he'd bothered for the past, oh, twenty-eight years.

He let the hood slam closed.

From his pocket, his phone rang. *Mom.* It had only been a few days since he'd talked to her last.

He accepted the call. "Morning." He leaned one hip against the truck's fender.

"I just got off the phone with Tina Davidson. Do you know what she just saw?"

His neighbor was one of the biggest gossips in town. It could be anything. Luckily, his mom didn't seem to expect an answer.

"She saw Stevie Flower pull into your drive. *Stevie Flower.*"

It wasn't funny how fast the gossip mill worked in Redbud Trails. Tina must've passed by his driveway no more than five minutes ago. Then she'd jumped right on the phone with his mom.

"We were friends back in high school." It was a half-truth.

"I don't care about high school. That girl is trouble. She's constantly in the tabloids about this scandal or that."

He bit back a harsh retort. His mother shouldn't be reading those rags. Nothing in them was true.

"Just two weeks ago, she went back into rehab!"

He snorted.

"Did she come straight from rehab to you? Is that the kind of influence you want around my *granddaughter?*"

Lily. He hadn't spared one thought for the impressionable five-year-old.

The farm was far enough out of Redbud Trails proper that he hadn't thought people from town would be gossiping about Stevie's presence, especially if she was only in town for a few days. But he also hadn't counted on Tina stirring things up so fast. And Lily didn't need any more complications in her life.

"I'll call you later, Mom." He hung up, knowing he'd have to listen to her gripe about his poor manners the next time they spoke.

He whirled for the house, realizing he hadn't warned Stevie about his niece. He'd been so caught up in the puzzle that was the woman that he hadn't spared Lily a thought.

He hit the back porch at a run and shoved through the door.

There was Stevie standing in the center of the kitchen with her duffel at her feet. Lily stood in the archway beyond, dressed and ready to go, like she'd been about to join him for his pumpkin wrangling.

"Stevie, I forgot to tell you about Lily."

"I didn't do anything," Lily chimed, her eyes wide.

That kind of statement was usually preceded by Lily *doing something* to get into trouble, but he didn't see anything amiss, only the two females standing there.

Stevie's back was to him, and as she slowly turned to look at him, her chin trembled. He saw the tears standing in her eyes and clumping her eyelashes.

"Your daughter?" Stevie whispered.

"My niece."

Lily came to his side silently, giving Stevie a wide berth. She reached for his hand and he gave it to her, allowing her to cling. They neither one knew what was going on, but Lily was astute enough to understand that something was wrong.

"Do you—?" he started

"I need to—" Stevie said, interrupting his lame attempt at comfort.

She scooped her bag off the floor and rushed into the hall toward the stairs, but not before he saw the tears spilling down her cheeks.

He stood there, struck dumb, wondering just what he'd gotten himself into.

Lily tugged on his hand. "Uncle Jake, what's wrong with her?"

"I don't know, Lilybean." He looked down and tweaked her nose with his opposite hand.

"Are we gonna help her?"

His chest expanded with pride. Lily was a born nurturer. Hated to see any person or animal hurting. And seeing her childlike compassion warmed him, but it was also his job to protect her.

"We're gonna try, Bean."

There was also a part of him that felt woefully unequipped to deal with whatever was going on with Stevie. He and Lily had a deal. She always told him what she was feeling. That way, he didn't have to try to figure it out—and fail.

Stevie probably wouldn't accept those terms.

Was his mom right? Had he let trouble walk through the back door?

Not to mention the massive amount of work he'd planned to accomplish over the next few days. It wasn't only Lily that was depending on him. Courtney was too, whether she'd admit it or not.

Just like in his studies, the most difficult problems often had no answers. Was Stevie going to be one of those?

STEVIE PRESSED a cool washcloth against her eyes, but it didn't stop the burning. Nor did it help the flames in her heart.

This was a mistake. It had to be.

Seeing Jake's niece had shaken her more than she could have anticipated. For a moment, in the shadowed hallway, she'd seen Sienna. When Lily had come further into the kitchen and the light had fallen across her face, Stevie saw she was very different from Sienna, younger —maybe five years old—and light where Sienna had been dark.

But the damage had been done. She'd been shaken and then made a fool of herself trying to get out of the room.

Her phone rattled from the counter where she'd set it. She glanced at the display. Zack again. She powered down the phone.

A board creaked in the hallway outside. Then a soft knock sounded on the door.

"Stevie?" Jake asked.

Noodles. She was going to have to face him.

She pressed the towel harder against her eyes, trying to breathe in deeply. It didn't help.

She lowered the towel and looked up into the mirror, gripping the cool counter with one hand. For a moment, she focused on the colorful pink and purple shower curtain reflected behind her. Then she forced her gaze to her face.

The tip of her nose was bright red, and her eyes were bloodshot, huge bags hanging under them. So much for the attraction she'd registered in Jake's face when she'd first arrived.

It shouldn't matter, but some latent sense of pride made it.

She moved to the door and opened it to find him standing out in the hall, hands in his pockets.

"Are you okay?" No doubt he was regretting letting her into his house.

She shook her head. She would never be okay again.

But he deserved some explanation, if she could get it out.

"I came here because..." Her voice emerged in a hoarse whisper, and she had to swallow back the knot in her throat. "In high school..."

Remembering what he'd lost back then brought fresh tears, and she took in a wavering breath. He was much closer than he'd been outside, and now when he stepped forward, he was *right there*. He reached out and clasped her elbow. She could feel warmth emanating from his touch, but somehow it didn't warm her.

"I lost someone," she forced out. "And I came because—"

Finally, the tears she'd been holding back came like a

storm, and she drew away from his touch to put both hands over her face.

He moved even closer—inappropriately close, but she didn't push him away. His hand came to rest on her back. Her shoulder nudged into his side. As an embrace went, it was awkward at best, but it was closer than anyone had been in months.

"And you knew I'd understand," he murmured, close to her ear.

He didn't sound angry.

"I know you c-can't fix it," she choked out. No one could. Sienna was gone, and it was her fault. Grief spiraled.

He held her for a long time. He was perfectly still, not rubbing her back or making annoying platitudes. Just breathing and holding her.

At last, she was able to wipe her eyes. As she straightened, his hand fell away from her back, and he stepped away.

He rubbed the back of his neck. "I've got work that has to be done today. I'll have some time to talk after supper..."

She nodded. "I might try to sleep."

His eyes softened. "If you wake up and want to come out later, you're welcome."

She nodded again, thankful that he really did seem to understand what she needed. He wasn't pushing.

He was just there.

CHAPTER 2

*W*ith the afternoon sun bright overhead, Jake watched Stevie and Lily pile small pumpkins into a cardboard box. They were standing in the field of harvested pumpkins, in a field a quarter mile behind the house. The girls seemed all right, so he quit looking and started back to work, hauling two basketball-sized pumpkins to the flatbed trailer he'd attached to the farm truck.

It'd gotten warm enough that he'd shed his flannel shirt earlier. He'd caught Stevie eyeing his T-shirt, which had Newton's Law of Cooling printed on it. He might as well have worn a *kick the nerd* sign on his chest.

He and the girls had spent all afternoon hauling the gourds from the field to the barn and carefully packing the smaller ones in boxes. Over the next couple of days— the entirety of his break from teaching at the university —he'd send some of the pumpkins to locals who frequented different farmers' markets. The rest he'd sell from here, like he did the peaches and blackberries they grew throughout the summer months. He'd built a little open shelter off the front of the barn and hired some teens from town to handle the cash exchange a few afternoons a week.

Stevie hadn't slept. She'd been inside for maybe thirty minutes before she'd joined him and Lily out by the barn.

From his own experience, he'd guess that grief overwhelmed her if she tried to relax enough to get to sleep. He'd been there once, after he'd lost his brother. Jake had only been fifteen at the time, his first experience with gut-wrenching grief.

Once she'd told him why she was there, everything had fallen into place, like finding a clever change of variables in an equation. For a brief window, he'd believed she'd come to him because she missed him. That somehow, she regretted what had happened *that day*.

But it hadn't been that at all. She'd remembered that he'd lost his brother.

Everything was clear now, but it still stung a little that his hopeful hypothesis had been wrong.

At least this way he knew what the expectations were up front—on his end, he'd offer her friendship and what comfort he could.

THE LATE AFTERNOON breeze ruffled Stevie's hair. The sun was a huge sinking ball at the horizon, and shadows lengthened. It had cooled significantly since she'd come out in a long-sleeved T-shirt and jeans earlier. She'd tried to lie down for a bit, but the moment she'd closed her eyes, grief crowded in.

"One more load," Jake called out.

Stevie picked up a pumpkin the size of her first TV and trudged to the flatbed trailer to deposit it.

No doubt her back and legs would be aching tomorrow, but something about the physical effort felt...right.

Nearby, Lily piled teensy baby pumpkins into a cardboard box. She'd filled probably twenty others like it as they'd worked all afternoon.

It certainly wasn't ground-breaking work. It was repetitive, filling and re-filling the trailer, then unloading the pumpkins and sorting them into piles in front of the barn.

Jake was a pumpkin farmer.

It was bizarre.

She passed Jake as he carried two large pumpkins to the trailer. The muscles in his bare arms stood out in stark relief. She swallowed hard and looked away.

The trailer's surface was already more than three-quarters full. They were almost done.

Within minutes, they'd loaded the trailer full of pumpkins, and Jake settled Lily onto the back of the trailer.

Stevie stood on her tiptoes and pushed her rear up onto the trailer.

Jake glanced at her and nodded, then moved to get in the truck, leaving Lily—sort of—in her care. Would he do that, if he knew?

Moments later, the truck started with a low growl

and a burst of exhaust that momentarily overpowered the fresh air and ripe pumpkins.

The truck audibly kicked into gear, and Jake started off at a slow roll back toward the house and barn.

She breathed in deeply, enjoying the scent of the grass and the land and the sharp scent of autumn.

The farmland breathed life back into her in the quiet moments as she rode beside a silent Lily on the back of the trailer. Grasses brushed her feet but not Lily's as Jake navigated around the corner of the peach orchard toward the barn.

Being out here soothed her. Sienna would have loved it.

The jagged brokenness in Stevie's chest opened wide, and she swallowed rapidly.

"Didja bring your guitar?" Lily asked. "Uncle Jake said you're a singer." The little girl had barely spoken to Stevie all day, but Stevie had heard the girl chattering to her uncle. Probably Stevie had scared her with her meltdown in the kitchen earlier.

"No, I didn't." Where usually she heard music in everything, all of that had shut down since she'd received the news.

"We listen to your songs sometimes on the radio." The girl's head tilted to one side as she assessed Stevie. "You're a good worker."

The abrupt change in topic surprised Stevie. She exhaled sharply, stifling the laugh that wanted to erupt. "Thanks." The little girl sounded so grown up.

She looked a lot like her uncle. Inquisitive blue eyes,

wavy blonde hair cascading from her ponytail. How had he come to have custody of Lily?

"I like helping uncle Jake. He works hard all the time. Even in the summer when everyone's off school."

Jake had been the same back in high school. He'd known what he wanted and worked hard—often working ahead—to get it.

"Do you like school?" Stevie asked. Sienna hadn't. Stevie had thought of homeschooling her. Taking her on the road. She'd been touring for more than five years. She'd grown accustomed to the long stretches on a tour bus. Figured it would be bonding time for them.

"I like my teacher," Lily said, breaking Stevie out of dangerous thoughts.

She welcomed the distraction.

One positive thing had resulted from coming here: her curiosity about Jake and his niece had allowed her to focus on something other than the tragedy she'd been running from.

STEVIE PAUSED at the first-floor landing, one hand on the stair railing. She could hear Jake and Lily's voices from the kitchen where they must have been preparing supper, if the banging pots and running water were any indication.

The afternoon had been...pleasant. The outdoors felt huge, wide enough for her to keep some distance from Jake and Lily. And the activity of hauling the pumpkins had given her hands something to do.

But the kitchen table would be small. Intimate. She wasn't sure she could face Jake and Lily across the dining room table without breaking into tears again.

She checked her phone out of habit. No new notifications. Zack had left two messages earlier, frustrated she'd disappeared.

Instead of joining Jake and Lily she wandered in the opposite direction. A large living room took up the east corner of the home. It had friendly windows on both corners. Mornings in here would be bright and cheerful. A TV was attached to the wall above the red-brick fireplace. A comfortable-looking L-shaped sofa bracketed the room. A soft throw was folded on top of one corner.

Across the coffee table were scattered several children's books. A pair of shoes hid between the coffee table and the sofa.

It was comfortable, lived-in.

She loved it. Felt at home here, not like the apartment she saw only a few weeks out of the year. Jake's place reminded her of the idyllic childhood that seemed so far away now. If only her mom and dad were still around. They might've understood her grief.

She turned her back on the living room and almost forced her feet to take her down the hall to the kitchen, but at the last second, she delayed again.

On the opposite side of the living room stood French-style doors, which led to another room. One of the doors was slightly ajar, and she slipped inside, flipping on the light to disperse the shadows.

It was Jake's office.

Here was the piece of the man she'd been missing since this morning. A large oak desk sat in one corner, angled so he had a view of both the picture window that looked out over the property and the doors—no doubt he sometimes worked in here while Lily played in the living room. A full bookshelf spanned the wall behind the desk, which was bare except for the closed laptop.

She had a strange urge to look in the drawers. She'd bet every pencil was in place. She didn't give in to the urge, only allowing herself to touch the corner of his desk. It was cool and solid.

Along the far wall hung three huge whiteboards, covered in equations. She couldn't make heads or tails of it, but her eyes traced the lines of letters and numbers and symbols she didn't even recognize.

Movement from the hallway turned her head. Jake was there, his eyes assessing from behind his glasses.

"I found your office," she said.

"So you did."

"Are you just doing the farming, or...?"

Without the hat and in his stocking feet, he looked more like the teen she remembered. He riffled his hair with one hand. "I'm a professor at the university in Weatherford. Physics and freshman chemistry."

A small laugh burbled out. Followed by a sharp pain just behind her breastbone.

Was that the first time she'd laughed since Sienna's death?

He seemed to understand her swinging emotions and waited while she breathed through the pain.

"You're a professor." She cleared her throat when the words wanted to stick. Of course he was. "So when you said you were on fall break, you meant the both of you."

"Yep."

She nodded to the whiteboards. "And that's something you're working on in your spare time?"

"Something like that."

She wondered how many papers he'd authored. Was he a PhD? There was no plaque on the wall, but he wasn't pretentious like that. And anyway, something like that would probably hang on the wall of his office at the university.

"It looks—"

"Nerdy."

She smiled, and again, the feeling felt abnormal after so many tears. "I was going to say *amazing*. Or maybe *intense*."

His mouth twisted to one side, as if *intense* were an insult rather than a compliment.

"You got me through Mr. Pearson's class," she reminded him.

A light in his eyes dimmed.

It bothered her. "Why aren't you down at OU, or even...Berkeley. Isn't that one of the cutting edge schools for physics?"

"I've got commitments here. And there's always the Internet when I need to consult with someone long-distance."

He jerked his head toward the kitchen, indicating the

conversation was over. "We shouldn't leave Lily to her own devices for too long. You coming?"

She was the guest in his house, which left her little choice but to follow.

In the kitchen, Lily was standing on a chair at the counter, working away. As she neared, Stevie saw the girl was decorating three personal-sized pizzas, making smiley faces out of pepperonis.

"Do you like pepperoni, Miss Stevie?" the girl asked.

"Love it."

"It's our favorite." Lily turned from the counter with a flourish and wobbled on the edge of the stool. Jake was right there to catch her, slinging his arm around her waist and whirling her in a circle with a whoop before he set her on her feet.

He mussed Lily's hair, then gave her a gentle push out of the way before he opened the oven and slid the pizza pan in.

The girl whirled to music in her own head, bringing a lump to Stevie's throat. She cleared it with a *harrumph*. "Can I set the table?"

"Sure," Lily said. "I'll show ya where the plates are."

The little girl grabbed Stevie's hand, and she jumped at the contact. Lily didn't seem to notice as she tugged Stevie to the cabinet just to the side of the kitchen window.

"Up there."

The girl let go, and Stevie instantly missed the contact of that sweaty little hand.

As she reached for three plates, Lily opened a nearby drawer, and silverware clinked.

They went to the dining room table, which seated six, and set out the plates where Lily advised her to. The girl wanted them all to sit at one end of the table. Close. Like a family.

Jake brought in a large bowl of salad and two bottles of dressing.

"Uncle Jake says we should eat our veggies first."

Stevie's glance went to the man. "Does that make them more palatable?"

"Sometimes," he returned. "If they're cooked and you eat them while they're warm, they won't get slimy." He pulled out Stevie's chair for her as Lily slid into the seat at the head of the table. "Pizza should be done by the time you ladies finish your salads." He sat down across from Stevie. On the wall behind him hung a series of photos of him and Lily together in different poses. Some serious with real smiles, and some silly. Her eyes caught on the furthest, where it appeared Lily had wrestled her uncle to the ground atop a quilt. The photographer had caught them both mid-laugh.

"Are we gonna make something slimy at the Halloween party tomorrow night?" Lily asked, bringing Stevie's focus back to the meal.

Jake's head tipped to the side as he considered his niece. "Maybe."

"Our Halloween party is so fun, even though it's not Halloween night yet." Lily's words bubbled over as Jake dished out a good-sized portion of baby spinach leaves, green lettuce, and matchstick carrots onto her plate. "Uncle Jake is the mad scientist, and all my friends think he's sooo funny."

"A mad scientist, huh?" Stevie crunched into her bite of salad.

She was surprised to see the tips of Jake's ears turn red. Was he embarrassed by Lily's gushing?

"This is only the second year I'm doing it—it's fun for the kids." He seemed to be defending himself. "We've sold pumpkins the last four years, and lots more of the local farmers bought their pumpkins here last year instead of at the super store over in Weatherford."

"Why do you farm if you've got a job teaching?" Stevie asked. She'd have thought a professor's salary would be plenty for the two of them to live on.

"My mom's coming home soon," Lily said. "And the pumpkin harvest and the peaches and blackberries are a nice sup-supplemental income."

Coming home?

The second part of Lily's sentence sounded like she'd heard it repeated time and time again, but Stevie's thoughts fixed on the first part. She'd been out of town for too long. If she'd stayed, she'd surely know what the girl meant—Redbud Trails was notorious for its gossip— but Stevie hadn't a clue.

Jake caught her eye and shook his head slightly. Whatever it was, he didn't want to talk about it in front of Lily.

"I'll go check on the pizzas." Jake pushed back from the table and returned to the kitchen.

27

"Uncle Jake said you were friends when you were in school," Lily said. She fiddled with her fork, not eating her salad.

"We were." They'd been peripheral friends, mostly becoming close when he'd tutored her.

"I've got lotsa friends, but Avery is my best friend."

The girl didn't seem to stop talking.

Stevie looked at Lily's plate, where the girl was scooting pieces of her food around with her fork. She must really dislike vegetables.

Then Stevie realized what Lily was doing. The carrot pieces outlined a face and slashed a smile. Lily had used two olives for eyes, and lettuce made up the hair.

"Do you like making faces with your food?" And did Jake allow it?

"I like art," Lily said simply, concentrating on her plate. "I'm good at it."

Was this what supper with Sienna would've been like? The thought closed Stevie's throat, and she had to set her fork on the table.

She'd gone the last five—maybe ten minutes without thoughts of Sienna intruding. Was it a betrayal of everything she was grieving to enjoy this supper with Lily?

Her emotions were so confused, so raw that she didn't know what was right anymore.

Only that Sienna should be here with her, and she wasn't.

CHAPTER 3

*J*ake took a sweep through the downstairs after he'd put Lily to bed. He gathered up a puffy princess skirt, a bright yellow stocking cap, and a pair of goggles from the living room couch—the remains of two discarded Halloween costumes she'd decided against. Lily's boots were a tripping hazard in the hallway, and he picked them up too.

The rambunctious five-year-old had been worn out from the day's work—although not too worn out to get in a water fight with him at bath time.

She'd also been alert enough after story time to ask him if Stevie was going to be his girlfriend.

He'd choked on nothing but air and spit, and she'd watched from beneath her quilt.

"No," he'd assured her quickly, though not without a disgruntled *whump* of his heart against his ribcage.

He had planned to grade some of the mid-term tests he'd brought home with him from the university, but he'd check on Stevie first. He'd rejoined the girls after taking the pizzas out of the oven to find Stevie quiet and teary. He wished he knew more about what was going on with her. Was it a child she was grieving? A friend? She'd reacted more to Lily than she had to him.

He was tempted to boot up his laptop and do a search for current news about Stevie and her life, but he feared that would make him no better than his mother, confusing gossip rags with truth.

Instead, he poured two mugs from the coffeepot he'd brewed after dinner and went in search of Stevie.

Somehow he knew she wouldn't be sleeping, even though she'd driven through the night and worked all afternoon.

He found her curled on a rocker on the porch, wrapped in the afghan he usually kept folded on the living room couch. Her face was turned up toward the stars, but she wasn't stargazing, not really.

He didn't know whether she was ready to talk about what had happened. When his brother had died, it had been months before he could talk about Adam with anyone. But she'd sought him out for a reason.

He sat in the rocker adjacent to her, offered her the coffee.

"Thank you," she said softly. Their fingers brushed as she accepted the mug.

He felt a very familiar tug in the region of his heart, but he pushed it away. She hadn't been interested back then, and he hadn't changed since high school. He was still a physics geek. He even wore a lab coat when the occasion required.

She wasn't just out of his league, she was in another dimension entirely.

And she'd come to him for comfort. Nothing more. That's what he had to remember.

He stretched his legs out in front of his rocker and crossed them at the ankles. "Sometimes I think about what Adam would be like now."

Saying the words opened up the hollow place in his heart. The pain remained, but it wasn't as sharp as it had been in those early days. Adam had been gone for thirteen years, the victim of a fast-growing, incurable cancer.

He felt Stevie's eyes on him, but he didn't look at her. He sipped his coffee and gazed at the stars. The moon had already passed behind the house, and the sky was a blanket of heavenly lights. A neighbor's cow lowed, the far-off sound mournful. Or maybe that was fanciful thinking.

His voice was slightly hoarse when he continued. "He would have spoiled Lily rotten. You think her room's full of dolls and stuff now? Adam always did everything over the top. He'd probably have built her a life-sized dollhouse out back."

Adam had been two years older than Jake. They'd had their moments of sibling rivalry, but he'd been Jake's best friend.

"If he'd been here, he could've reined Courtney in."

Jake didn't mean for the words to sound accusing, not really. Lily's mother was the youngest of the three siblings. She'd been thirteen when Adam had died, twenty when Lily had been born.

"What happened with Courtney?" Stevie asked. He'd sensed her curiosity at the supper table, but it wasn't something he liked to talk about in front of Lily.

"She wasn't interested in college. She was working as a home-health aide and..." He sighed, pressure tightening his chest. "She was caught selling prescription painkillers. Her five-year sentence is up in the spring."

He glanced at her. Without the overhead light on, it was hard to read her expression, but he imagined he could see her doing mental calculations.

"She had Lily while she..."

"Was in prison. Yes." He still remembered Courtney's tears when he'd seen her briefly at the hospital to take custody of Lily. She'd only gotten to hold her daughter for a couple of hours, and he'd seen that the pain of separation was tearing Courtney apart. It had altered his sister—for the better. While she'd been a wild child during high school and after, now she'd changed her ways.

"Does Lily know? About where her mom is?"

His chest tightened, as if his insides had begun exerting a gravitational pull all their own. "I've told her that her mom can't be here right now but that she really wishes she could be. I mean...she's five. Five year olds see things in black and white. Princesses and Evil Queens."

"So Lily doesn't visit her mom?"

He shook his head. "I go down there about once a month to check in with Courtney. She's the one who asked me not to bring Lily to the prison. She didn't want Lily to see her like that."

"Wow."

Tell him about it. He didn't know that he agreed with his sister's choice, but he hadn't forced the issue. His coffee gone, the breeze was chilly enough that he wished he were sharing that afghan with Stevie. He crossed his arms instead.

"And Lily's dad?"

"Dead."

"And what about your parents?"

"They moved to Florida after Courtney's high school graduation. I didn't get all of the details, but I guess when Courtney called collect to tell them about the baby, they claimed they weren't interested in being parents again."

"So it's just been you and Lily since she was born."

"Yep."

"Wow," she said again. "What were you, twenty-two?"

"Twenty-three. And stupid-scared." He set his now-empty coffee mug on the railing in front of him. "I'd never even held a baby before. Or installed a carseat."

She was smiling softly, her gaze far-off.

"And then...I held her for the first time. I looked down into that little face, and I loved her. I didn't know it then, but Lily was the best thing that ever happened to me." He smiled. "Even through the terrible twos."

All of a sudden, Stevie's cup clattered to the porch. She bent double, her hands covering her face. She sobbed, shoulders shaking with the force of her emotions.

Jake sat frozen. He knew his words had triggered this breakdown, and he even knew she probably *needed* a good cry, but he didn't know if she'd welcome his comfort.

"Mm—mm—mm—"

Was she humming? No, she was trying to say something through her tears.

She gasped in a breath. "Mm-my little g-girl's name was S-Sienna."

Her words registered, and a phantom, sympathetic pain sliced through him. *Her little girl.*

He couldn't hold back. He went to his knees in front of her rocking chair and put his arms around her shoulders. And held her. And she let him.

CHAPTER 4

*S*tevie woke the next morning to sunlight streaming across her pillow.

How late was it?

The spare bedroom Jake had tucked her into was at the back of the house. She could barely hear muffled noises from downstairs.

This house, this room felt like...home. She was burrowed beneath an heirloom quilt. Lacy curtains hung in the window, and a dark-stained hope chest stood beneath it. How had Jake managed to make it this homey, this welcoming? Was there a woman in his life?

She sat up, stretching one arm above her head. A giant yawn cracked her jaw.

Her face felt hot and swollen to the touch from all the crying she'd done last night.

But she'd slept without dreaming, without waking in the night crying out for Sienna. For the first time since she'd received the news of Sienna's death.

It was a miracle, and she knew who'd worked it.

Jake.

Jake and his tender embrace.

She should probably be embarrassed that she'd broken down and blubbered all over the man—and she did mean *all* over the man. The shoulder of his shirt had been drenched with her tears. But all she felt was...lighter.

Oh, her grief wasn't gone. She could still feel it bubbling just beneath the surface.

But her tears had cleansed her of some of the most jagged edges.

Jake hadn't tried to offer false comfort. Hadn't told her it would be okay. They both knew it wouldn't. He'd opened their conversation by mentioning Adam and Courtney, a conversation she somehow knew he wouldn't have with just anyone.

His openness had been the catalyst, a road sign directing her toward healing.

She wanted to repay him in some tangible way. Instinctively, she knew he would reject it if she offered cash for letting her stay. But this was supposed to be his break, and the farm work seemed never-ending. Maybe she could find a way to help him get ready for his mad scientist event tonight.

Imagining Jake as a crazy, wild-haired scientist made her smile. He was just the opposite. Rugged. Well-spoken. A softie when it came to Lily.

She got out of bed and padded down the hall to the bathroom. One look in the mirror, and she winced. Her hair was wild, sticking up all over. Her eyes had cleared somewhat, but the skin just beneath was puffy and pink. She didn't think she'd packed enough makeup to cover those bags.

A ten-minute shower had her feeling more like her normal self—but what was her new normal going to be?

She couldn't have Sienna in her life. But somehow she couldn't go back to the extensive touring and producing and recording that her schedule demanded.

Her phone beeped with an email from Zack. He'd forwarded her a link to an online tabloid article. Somehow, they'd turned the fact that she'd blown off one tour stop into speculation that she was in rehab again.

She'd never even been once. Seen enough careers ruined when people used drugs, so she didn't. Where did the writers get this stuff?

It was one more reason she couldn't go back to Nashville. What was she going to do now?

There were no answers to be found hiding upstairs, so she went down.

She found Jake and Lily in the kitchen again. Lily sat at the nook table this morning, working on a plate of pancakes and scrambled eggs. "Ha, Spevie," the girl said through a mouthful of food.

"Manners, Lily. Morning," Jake said over his shoulder from his spot at the stove.

"Morning," she murmured, hesitating at the threshold.

"Coffee's on, and I've about got your plate filled."

She thought about arguing that he didn't have to wait on her, but her mouth was already watering from the aromas. She approached the counter, where an empty orange mug with a jack-o-lantern face waited.

Jake turned to her, and she couldn't help the blush that heated her face. Last night had been the first time in a long time she'd been held by a man. The last person she'd dated had been Zack, and that experience had turned her off of dating. Somehow, she and Zack maintained a somewhat tumultuous working relationship. And before Zack, she'd had a string of horrible first dates.

She tore her gaze away from Jake's face and then caught sight of his apron. It was black with *Zombies hate fast food* scrawled across the front. She laughed.

"Don't mess with the chef," he warned, but he flipped a pancake onto her plate anyway.

She poured the coffee and accepted the plate, then sat next to Lily.

She was reaching for the syrup when she looked down at her plate. The pancakes were shaped like pumpkins and even had the eyes and mouth cut out like jack-o-lanterns. Across the table, Lily's pancakes were decorated with chocolate spiderwebs, and her scrambled eggs appeared to have been murdered by ketchup.

"Has anyone ever told the two of you that you take Halloween too seriously?" It was still ten days away, but they were all about it.

Jake sat down caddy-corner to Lily with a clank of his plate against the table. He and the child shared a glance that spoke volumes, and then he looked at Stevie. "We have no idea what you're talking about."

Stevie shook her head and forked a bite of pancakes in her mouth. Flavors exploded over her tastebuds. She let her eyes fall closed and chewed more slowly. "Mmm."

Lily started to giggle.

She opened her eyes to find Jake watching her with an expression she couldn't decipher. His eyes glittered behind his glasses.

"These are really good. How'd you get the pumpkin flavor in there?"

He cleared his throat. "I used a little pumpkin in the batter."

"Wow. You're a good cook, too." He'd been constantly surprising her since she'd arrived yesterday morning.

How was it that a man like him wasn't married off with three kids of his own?

She nipped that wayward thought in the bud. "So what're we working on today? Please don't say lugging around more pumpkins." She made a show of rubbing her lower back.

"Are you really hurt?" Lily asked.

"Oh no," she assured the little girl quickly. "I just don't use my lifting muscles very often on tour." At least, not anymore. In the early days, she and her bandmates unloaded and set up and tore down and re-loaded for every gig. Now she had roadies for all that.

"You're in luck," Jake said. "Today we're setting up the experiments in the barn. And I'll probably field a few shipments to local sellers."

"Ooh, are we gonna get to try the experiment early?" Lily asked. "Please, please please?"

Jake tweaked her nose. "Depends. How fast can you finish your breakfast?"

Lily started shoveling pancakes and eggs into her mouth at an even faster rate.

"Hey, slow down!" Jake told her on a laugh.

Stevie watched the interplay between uncle and niece and couldn't help the lingering thought. Why *didn't* Jake have a wife?

STEVIE SEEMED MORE STEADY TODAY. Jake found himself stealing glances as she and Lily wiped off the outdoor picnic tables he'd positioned end-to-end in the barn. Dust motes swirled in the warm morning sunlight.

The open space rang with their laughter and Lily's off-key singing of a song she'd learned in school. Stevie didn't join in.

The previous owners of the farm had kept horses in here, but over the last two summers, he'd disassembled one side of stalls, leaving a huge open area.

With the large double doors on both ends thrown wide, the space was open and welcoming and perfect for his needs.

He'd set up a raised platform on one end, so that later tonight, he could demonstrate for the kids. Their parents would be there to help, but he'd done this last year, and it had worked well.

Stevie paused, and he saw her check her phone. Was real life calling? He'd seen her tour schedule last year, full of concerts in cities across the U.S. She'd have to go back eventually. But how soon?

She stuffed the phone back into her pocket with a frown. "What now, captain?"

"Oh, can we do the experiment?" Lily pleaded.

He squinted at his niece. "Isn't it about nap time for little girls?"

"Aw, Uncle Jake, I'm too big for naps."

That's what she said every day.

"Hmm..." He winked at Stevie. "I guess we could skip nap time today...if I can stay awake. Let's take a break." He could finish cleaning off the tables and sorting supplies after Lily had a little fun.

He set an armful of plastic tablecloths on the farthest table and took one off the top.

He brought it to Stevie and Lily at their table and began unfolding it. Stevie met him and took the other end of the tablecloth and they shook it out together.

For a second, her face disappeared behind the plastic, and then reappeared, her blue eyes shining at him. Travel and the media and all of that might be a part of her reality, but for today, he could pretend that she was part of his.

They lowered the tablecloth and smoothed it in place. Lily was already on her knees on the bench seat, and she banged on the now-covered table.

"What're we making, Uncle Jake?"

"How does goop sound, kiddo?"

Goop? Stevie mouthed.

He walked across the barn to one of the wheelbarrows he'd lined up in front of his makeshift stage. Stevie met him there. He tried not to react to her presence at his elbow, but couldn't help the way the hair on the back of his neck rose.

He handed her two plastic measuring cups and a gallon jug of water and sent her back to Lily at the table. He grabbed a few things and brought his load to the table.

"Glue?" Lily asked.

"Yep. First, pour one cup of water into your measuring cup."

Stevie had set her things on the table and stepped away.

Lily looked at her. "Aren't you going to do the experiment with me?"

Stevie's eyes darkened, but she smiled a trembling smile. "If you want me to."

She settled at the table next to Lily. He sat across from them, content to let them work through the project. It would be a good gauge to see whether the kids tonight would be able to do the project.

Stevie steadied both measuring cups as Lily poured.

Jake guided them to add a teaspoon of Borax detergent to each cup of water. The soapy scent momentarily overtook the dirt and outdoorsy smells that surrounded them.

"Now what?" Lily asked.

"Now pour your glue into the empty bowl."

Lily's face lit. "All of it?"

He nodded.

3 DAYS WITH A COWBOY

Stevie helped her unscrew the tops of both bottles of glue.

"My teacher doesn't like it if we get glue all over the place," Lily said as she poured a thick stream of glue into the bowl.

Stevie looked up at him, her lips twitching. "I bet that's why your uncle put down the tablecloth." She nudged her bottle toward Lily. "You can do mine, too."

"Thanks!" Lily's tongue stuck out of the corner of her mouth as she squeezed the glue bottle. "Do you got a boyfriend, Miss Stevie?"

Now Stevie's eyes darted to him and away. "No. Do you have a boyfriend?"

"Nuh-uh. Uncle Jake says I can't have a boyfriend until I'm twenty-five."

"Hmm. That sounds a little overprotective," Stevie said. But when her eyes slid up to meet his again, he thought there was a hint of admiration inside.

"I have lotsa friends who are boys, though." She set the glue bottle on the table, where it promptly fell on its side. "All done!"

"We want to add a little water to the glue," he said. "And some food coloring. What color goop do you want to make?"

"Purple!" Lily cheered gleefully.

"Hmm. I've got primary colors," Jake said. "Does anybody know what two colors combine to make purple?"

Lily and Stevie conferred with bent heads, and then Lily chimed, "Blue and red!"

Stevie helped her squirt the food coloring into the glue mixture, and they stirred it with plastic spoons he'd brought over. Stevie added red to her own bowl.

"Now dump the soapy water in."

He waited for Lily's reaction, and it came as the Borax water hit the glue. The chemical reaction was instantaneous, forming solids in the larger bowl.

"Cool!" Lily's excitement was palpable.

"Now you've got to mix it until you have goop."

Stevie didn't seem so sure. Her nose wrinkled. "We have to touch it?"

"Oh yeah!" Lily immediately dug her hands into the bowl. She brought them up, and the nearly solid slime slid back into the bowl in long, melted-cheese-like strings. "This is *awesome!*"

Stevie tentatively put her hands in the mixture. "It's cold." She mushed her fingers around. Her focus was on her bowl as she said, "What about your Uncle Jake? Does he have a girlfriend?"

His ears got hot as Lily shook her head.

"Why not? He's older than twenty-five."

His chest warmed too. Was she fishing? Right. Wishful thinking. Stevie was probably just nosey, like his mother.

"Uncle Jake says I'm the most important woman in his life."

"Hmm." He felt the intensity of Stevie's gaze. Her hands were still in the goo, and he kept his eyes focused there. The compound was coming together.

What Lily had said was true. Sometimes ten o'clock

arrived, and he realized he'd forgotten to eat supper in the whirlwind of homework and re-packing backpacks for the next day, not to mention grading his students' work and preparing lectures. Life with a five-year-old wasn't conducive to dating. But there was also more to his excuse than a five-year-old needed to know.

"This is *so cool*, Uncle Jake!" Lily held up her purple gunk.

"Is there supposed to be liquid left in the bowl?" Stevie asked, and he was happy for the distraction.

"A little."

Stevie held up her gloppy, red goo. She squished it in her hands until it made burping noises that had Lily rolling with laughter.

"So what's your verdict? I'm going to be a hit tonight?"

He meant the question to ask whether the goop would be a hit with the kids, but when Stevie's eyes focused on him, he felt it in his gut.

Her eyes shone with mischief. "You're something, all right."

"DO YOU WANT TO TAKE A WALK?"

Stevie looked over her shoulder from where she'd been gazing out the kitchen window. Jake stood in the kitchen archway, one hand braced casually against the wall.

He looked like the consummate cowboy, his hair smashed and mussed from his Stetson. Only his glasses hinted at his profession. And the notation on the shirt beneath his open flannel again. Today, it read: $(-\infty, \infty)$ with the words "Get real" beneath.

"She fell asleep in front of the TV," he said with a jerk of his chin over his shoulder. Lily had worked a little but mostly played alongside him as he'd set up for his demonstration tonight.

Jake had taken several breaks when the local grocer, hardware store owner, and several other sellers had stopped by to pickup boxes of pumpkins. His business seemed to be thriving.

And Stevie had no doubt that the kids who showed up would be awed by the goop-making adventure. Lily certainly had been.

And she'd been a little awed by the cowboy who would go to such lengths to create fun for his niece. And to provide for his family. He hadn't said it outright, but she could guess what kind of persecution Courtney would face when she was released from prison. Likely, she'd be stuck in a low-paying job until—if—someone in town decided they could trust her with more responsibility. They wouldn't wait to see whether she'd changed her ways. They'd judge. Because it was a small town. Even if Courtney tried to relocate, the felony conviction would follow her on any job application and background check she had to go through.

She wondered what kind of adjustment Lily and Jake would go through when Courtney was released.

But Jake had taken the initiative and created sustainable income through the farm, income that the people of

Redbud Trails already supported. It would be a nice supplement to whatever job Courtney got.

The man wasn't just smart, he took care of his own.

"A walk sounds perfect," she said.

She followed him out the back door. The sun had passed its zenith, though there were still a couple hours until the mad scientist party.

He fiddled with his phone on the way down the steps. She watched him with unabashed curiosity. Zack's texts and calls had finally tapered off. She was relieved. She knew he wouldn't be silent forever—he could be tenacious as a bulldog—but she needed the break. She couldn't stay hidden on Jake's farm forever. But the thought of going back to Nashville filled her with panic.

Jake saw her watching and gave her a sheepish half-smile. He turned the screen so she could see it. It showed a sound bar and small upticks where it was picking up sound. Through the phone's speaker, she could hear soft breathing sounds. What in the world?

"It's a baby monitor app," he said as they started toward the peach trees planted in orderly rows at a distance behind the house. "Probably over-protective again, but this way if she wakes up disoriented or something, I'll be able to hear her."

It wasn't over-protective. It was just Jake.

"Why are you still single?"

He'd avoided the question earlier in the barn, but she was determined to discover the answer now. Jake was a family man. Had some woman broken his heart?

"It's no great mystery." He kicked at a tall tuft of grass as they meandered past.

He didn't offer more.

They passed beneath the first of the peach trees. Some leaves, not all, had fallen and crunched underfoot. The others rustled in the soft breeze.

"Is there a string of broken hearts in your past?" she asked.

She didn't want to admit why she was so curious. Their shared history was so limited, but since she'd arrived on his doorstep, he'd been kind. And she saw how he was with Lily.

"No broken hearts. I guess..." He rubbed the back of his neck with one hand. "I guess I've mostly been too intimidated to ask out the women I've been attracted to."

"Intimidated?" That made no sense. "But you're a PhD."

"Exactly. I'm a nerd."

A soft laugh bubbled out of her. "Don't most women like intelligent men?"

"Intelligent maybe. Not Sheldon Cooper."

She laughed again. "You're not like Sheldon. Maybe more Leonard."

He shook his head slightly, and she saw that he wasn't smiling. She stopped walking and placed a hand on his forearm. He stopped beside her.

"You have nothing to be intimidated about. You're a great guy."

He stared at the horizon. His mouth firmed into a straight line. Not really a frown, but not a smile either.

"C'mon," he said. He took off again, and she fell in step beside him.

They walked in silence beneath the half-bare branches of the trees. She breathed deeply, the crisp autumn air filling her lungs and the peace stitching up some of the jagged edges of her heart.

"I'd forgotten how it felt to just...be," she said softly.

His head turned slightly toward her. "You must have a busy schedule."

She nodded slowly. "Too busy." Her throat closed off. "I don't know if I can do it—be in the industry anymore."

She stopped again, turning away from Jake and toward the nearest tree. She sensed him stop behind her. She stepped closer to the tree and ran her fingertip along the trunk, the rough bark scratching her fingertip.

"Because of Sienna?" he asked.

Tears clogged her throat, and she nodded jerkily.

Last night she'd felt like a dam broke, and her tears had poured out. Today, it was her words she couldn't hold back.

"I met Sienna almost a year ago, at a charity event. My manager had organized a Thanksgiving visit to a girls' home in Nashville. Girls who were in the foster system, girls who didn't have foster families. It was supposed to be a photo op. Me behind the serving line, dishing up Thanksgiving dinner."

"She was this sassy little thing—" Her voice broke, and for a moment, she couldn't go on. She swiped at the tears that fell with the back of one hand.

She sensed Jake moving closer, but she kept her hand

on the tree, kept her face turned away from him.

"How old was she?"

She gulped back tears. "Seven."

He didn't push for more information. She spent long moments trying to catch her breath, trying to stem the tears.

"We just...connected. Something inside me recognized her, told me that she was supposed to be mine. I went home and called an attorney and started the process to try to adopt her."

She drew a shaky breath. "There were obstacles. Me being single. My lifestyle. Stupid tabloid lies. And there were family custody issues."

Fresh tears welled. "I only got to see her three times last year because I was so *busy*." Her breath rattled as she inhaled. "I should've pushed harder. Hired a tougher attorney. Petitioned the judge more often."

His hand cupped her shoulder. He remained behind her, and his presence steadied her. But the worst was still to come.

She didn't know if she could say it.

"She was playing in the yard—a yard with this huge wrought iron fence—when there was a drive-by shooting. She and another little girl were hit. Sienna died before the ambulance could arrive."

Saying the words took every last bit of her strength. But before she could collapse, Jake was there. With his hand on her shoulder, he guided her to turn around, and his arms came around her.

She sobbed against his chest, her hands fisted against

his shoulders.

It wasn't fair. Not fair that she'd lost Sienna, the girl she'd already thought of as her daughter. And...

It was her fault.

It was her fault.

She didn't realize she'd said the words out loud until one of Jake's hands cupped the back of her head. "It wasn't," he whispered fiercely.

"I sh-should've tried harder."

He didn't argue. Just held her close, let her pour out her grief and pain for the second time in less than twenty-four hours.

He was like a lighthouse in a storm. A rock that she could hold onto.

When she'd spent her tears, she leaned back the slightest amount. She'd pressed one hand against his neck in an instinctive, proprietary move.

She meant to apologize for crying all over him—again —or maybe turn away to hide the mess she knew her face had to be.

But instead, she found herself focused on his dear face. His lips.

She raised on tiptoes.

Maybe he bent his head to meet her, she couldn't be sure.

But suddenly her lips were brushing his. His kiss was warm and tender, like the man himself.

And she held on.

Until a soft voice emanated from his pocket. Lily, over the open phone connection. "Uncle Jake?"

CHAPTER 5

*J*ake stood beside Stevie next to the open barn doors as kids and parents streamed past them. Lily was running around, chattering with her friends and basically spreading excitement everywhere.

The moon was bright and high above them. Light spilled from the open barn doors and from the floodlight in the center of the yard.

He was intensely aware of Stevie at his elbow. Several folks greeted him, and her soft *hellos* echoed his. Some of them even recognized and hugged her. Some darted looks at her. He hoped they were simply curious.

His heart pounded hard in his chest whenever he thought of the kiss he and Stevie had shared. He thought of it almost constantly.

They'd kissed.

He wasn't kidding himself about what it meant. She'd been seeking comfort. And he'd met her kiss, offering it.

But...

But.

Her words from the afternoon swirled in his head. *You have nothing to be intimidated about.*

He kept reminding himself that she'd come here to run away from her life—a life that expected her back. She'd been desperate for someone to understand her grief.

That was all.

And again, there was that *but*...

Two families were getting out of their vehicles, and he figured just about everyone was here when one last pair of headlights turned up the drive. He squinted into the lights, trying to identify the vehicle. It was compact. Out of place, like Stevie's little hybrid had been yesterday morning.

Three little terrors—triplets that belonged to his friend Callum, raced past, and Jake was shaking Callum's hand when the newest arrival got out of the car.

Stevie's sharp intake of breath had Jake turning toward her. Her gaze was fixed on whomever had just gotten out of the car.

Light from the barn spilled behind them, and he couldn't get a good look at the approaching man until he was just a few feet away.

"Zack," she said, and it wasn't a greeting. Her voice was flat. "What are you doing here?"

"You disappeared." It wasn't a real answer.

There was a pregnant pause, as if Stevie didn't know what to say.

"Jake, this is my business manager, Zack. Zack, my friend Jake."

Zack's face swiveled to Jake and, even in the low light, he could read the calculation in the other man's assessing gaze.

Jake shook his hand firmly but didn't say a word. He might not have been an expert on body language, but he could read tension in the set of Stevie's shoulders.

And Jake was also too aware of what he looked like. He'd added gel and mussed his hair until it stood on end in a pseudo-Einstein look. He'd donned a white lab coat from his closet and pulled out the bulky black glasses he'd worn back in college—still held together by duct-tape across the bridge.

"Can you give us a few minutes, bud?" the business manager asked. It wasn't really a question.

Jake looked at Stevie.

"It's fine," she murmured. Her eyes seemed to beg him not to leave her alone, but the words didn't cross her lips, so he walked away reluctantly.

Not far, though. He slipped into the shadows close to the barn door. She'd called him her friend—no matter what he wanted after this afternoon—and her friend he would be. And right now, as her friend, he wasn't leaving her alone with that guy.

Her arms had crossed over her middle, her hands clutching her elbows as if she were holding herself together by sheer will alone.

Her face. That expression. It was the same one she'd

worn when she'd looked at him *that day*—a mixture of panic and uncertainty.

Back then, he'd figured she'd wanted to run away, and seeing her expression again reinforced that impression.

The business manager blasted her. "What are you doing out here in the middle of nowhere? You've already blown off four tour dates. Are you trying to get sued?"

She didn't move, but her stillness spoke volumes.

"How'd you find me?" Her voice was small, not like the boisterous giggles she'd shared with Lily earlier.

His lips twisted in a sneer. "There's an app on your phone. I can track your location."

He'd been tracking her? That was beyond creepy.

She shivered, and Jake had to fight his urge to rescue her. He wasn't part of her music industry life. It wasn't his place.

"Look, I've done what I can for you," Zack said, "but you're about to implode your career."

"Maybe I don't want to come back," she whispered.

Zack made a disparaging noise. "For what? For this *cowpoke*?"

"He's my friend." Her voice came slightly stronger now, but her words were like a blow to Jake's gut. He'd always been in the *friend zone*.

More silence between them. A loaded silence.

"I can't believe you've let this setback derail you like this."

"Sienna wasn't a setback. She was going to be my daughter." Maybe the business manager couldn't hear it, but Stevie's voice was gaining even more strength.

"You should be over her by now."

That was the wrong thing to say to a grieving mother. "Please go."

There was Jake's invitation to join them, but before he could move in their direction, Lily rushed past him without noticing him.

"Stevie, Stevie! We're about to start, c'mon."

"I'm not leaving unless you're in the car with me," Zack said, his voice low and threatening.

"You can't leave, Stevie!" Lily's voice ranged toward whining. "We gotta make s'more goop."

But Stevie took it in stride, accepting Lily when his niece grabbed her hand and started pulling her toward the barn. "I'll call tomorrow, and we can talk through some options." The way she'd said it, it wasn't a question.

The girls slipped past him into the barn. He couldn't tell whether Stevie noticed him in the shadows. He stayed and watched until Stevie's manager got in his car and drove away.

He ducked into the barn, loud with voices and humming with expectation. And then he was too busy being the mad scientist to talk to Stevie.

But it didn't stop him from having flashbacks to that terrible day in his sophomore year even as he hammed it up in front of the kids and took them through the steps of their experiment.

It was a good thing he'd gone through it with Stevie and Lily earlier, because now he could put himself on autopilot as those memories cut jagged holes in his world.

The weekend before *the event*, they'd had a marathon study session at the library. He could still smell the scent of thousands of books. Feel the hush that had surrounded them. They sat at a study table in the back corner of the library, and since it was a Saturday morning, they were the only students there.

Their knees bumped under the table. Again. This was the twelfth time it had happened.

He'd counted.

Even after weeks of tutoring, he constantly wiped sweaty palms against his jeans. And prayed she didn't notice.

They'd been working on Coulomb's Law, and her head was bent over the textbook splayed on the table before her. Her nose almost touched the page, as if the closer she got, the more it might make sense.

"So the force between the particles is dependent on the distance between them?" She asked the question tentatively, as if afraid he was going to correct her.

"You've got it."

She looked up, using one hand to hold her bangs out of her face. Her eyes were shining at him.

"I...got it?" she whispered. Her other hand squeezed his, sending a jolt to his toes.

He'd known she could understand, and smiled goofily back at her, sharing the joy that bubbled right out of her.

The memory flitted away as the kids shouted their joy, goo everywhere. Jake needed to focus, but as he blinked, more memories overtook him.

That moment in the library, that touch, had been the

impetus that had given him the courage for what happened a few days later. That, and the grief he'd still been processing over Adam's death. Adam had been a proponent of *go big or go home*.

And Jake was a *test-the-hypothesis* kind of guy.

But he'd wanted to feel close to his brother and he'd thought... He'd *hoped*.

He could still remember the jitters that had had him practically bouncing on the balls of his feet as he'd waited for her in the hallway by her locker.

The final bell had rung forty-five seconds before. Lockers slammed, and kids talked all around him, but he was stationary. He'd asked his final period teacher if he could leave early, and since he hadn't missed a day of class since eighth grade, Mr. Hampton hadn't even blinked at the request.

Now he was hoping she wouldn't be able to see his hands shaking where he clutched the bright green poster board. His shaking was dislodging some of the glitter that he'd painstakingly used to spell "Go to prom with me, Stevie?" It covered the toes of his shoes.

But he didn't have time to do anything about it.

There she was. She'd just turned the corner from her last period class and was approaching. She hadn't seen him yet. Her head was turned toward her friend Cara as they chatted.

His heart pounded. *She had to say yes.*

Didn't she?

Cara caught sight of him first. He couldn't decipher the widening of her eyes or the twitch of her lips.

He ran out of time to worry about it, because then, Stevie saw him too, and came to a halt a few feet away. "Oh. Jake."

And the look on her face was one he'd never seen before. That blend of panic and the dart of her eyes like she wanted to run, and the discomfort...

The words he meant to say stuck behind his Adams' apple. "Hey, Stevie. How'd the test go?"

His face burned.

How'd the test go? That wasn't what he'd wanted to ask, even if it was what they'd worked toward for all these weeks.

Now people were gathering behind her, whispering. Some were pointing at him.

"Um, I think it went okay. I don't think I'll need more tutoring." She looked away. For the second time, he thought she wanted to escape.

The probability of a favorable outcome was rapidly shrinking.

There was a roaring in his ears. This hadn't gone anything like he'd planned. He'd thought she would catch sight of him, and her face would light up, like that moment when she'd *gotten* Coulomb's Law.

He turned on his heel. And he was the one who ran away.

The memory burned a hole in his gut. The kids were done with their goop—Callum's triplets were peeling chunks off theirs and throwing it at each other—and he hopped off the makeshift stage.

"You are the coolest uncle ever!" Lily crowed. She

threw herself at him and wrapped her arms around his middle.

But after Stevie's visit from her business manager and the memories that had rushed back in, he found he couldn't quite meet Stevie's eyes.

STEVIE STOOD on the back porch, head cranked back to take in the night sky.

She couldn't believe Zack had come. At least he hadn't been able to bully her into rushing back to Nashville.

After the chaos of the evening—personal and physical —Lily had asked Stevie to tuck her in. She hadn't been able to refuse the girl, and now she wiped away the errant tear that she'd been able to hold off until now. She'd never had a bedtime with Sienna.

The brisk evening breeze cooled the tears on her cheeks.

The barn light was still on.

She crossed the yard. Even in the dark, she knew her way. Knew how to avoid the huge hole close to where Jake parked the farm truck. She was comfortable here. It felt like home.

She found Jake inside, still working. She paused in the doorway, lingering there, and he didn't seem to see her.

He was taking time at each table to wrap up the used tablecloth covered in goop and goo-making liquids and stuffing them in a trash barrel. He must've already gathered up all the bowls and measuring spoons, because they were stacked in neat little bundles along the front edge of the platform.

Music was playing. Music she recognized. Her own voice wafted quietly through the air, and she followed the sound of it to an old-school boom box, complete with cassette player, at the back of the stage.

"I can't believe you're listening to this. Where did you get it?"

He was playing one of the first songs she'd recorded. She'd scraped together enough money to pay for studio space and to have several boxes full of cassettes produced. She'd sold them out of the trunk of her car for months, mailed copies to music producers, and eventually she'd connected with her first manager.

She'd thought she'd tracked down and destroyed all the existing copies.

"I bought it off eBay a few years ago." He didn't look up.

His admission floored her.

"You aren't exactly my target audience." She walked to the table at the end of the line and began helping. The sooner the barn was cleaned up, the sooner they could get to bed. Tonight, she actually might sleep again. Between working with Jake for two days and the emotional roadblocks she'd busted through—not to mention facing off with Zack—she was physically and mentally spent.

He shrugged. "Doesn't stop me from enjoying your stuff."

But this was so different from her sound now. This

was nothing more than an acoustic guitar and her voice. The naive lyrics had been written when she was nineteen. She could hear every crack of the guitar strings, every note that she missed by a half-step. She hadn't done any retakes—couldn't afford them with what the studio had charged.

She shuddered in half-joking horror as she passed by Jake. "I can't believe you willingly listen to this. It's awful."

"It's you." He didn't look at her when he said it.

In fact, he hadn't really looked her in the eye since she'd joined him.

Was he angry that Zack had showed up earlier? Make that two of them. She'd been irate, felt violated to learn that Zack had used her phone to track her down. It was a controlling move and just reinforced that she'd been right to end her romantic relationship with him.

She needed to fire him. The fact that he hadn't understood her loss just emphasized how big the disconnect was between them. The tracking thing was beyond the pale. She would fire him, once she left here.

The problem was, she was running out of time.

Zack was partly right. She couldn't leave her career in limbo forever. She had tour dates scheduled the following week. She couldn't cancel them without disappointing her fans and causing the venues to lose a lot of money.

But she had a major problem.

"I haven't been able to sing since I got the phone call that Sienna had died," she admitted.

She kept her focus on the next table, on the next visit

to the trashcan. There was something freeing about the admission, but she also didn't want him to think less of her either.

And then the last table was cleared, and she had no choice but to face him. He met her near the corner of the stage. His eyes were soft, the way they'd been just before they'd shared that amazing kiss in the orchard. Her stomach pitched.

"Have you tried writing a song for her?" he asked.

She shook her head slightly. "I...can't. That part of me is blocked off somehow. I can't hear the music inside anymore."

He reached for her. She expected him to draw her in close again, but he only held her elbows loosely. There were still inches between them.

THE CASSETTE CLICKED OFF, leaving only silence.

Jake's heart pounded so loudly that she could probably hear it. His ears were burning.

He wanted to pull her closer.

But the image of her face when her business manager had appeared was etched into the front of his brain, superimposed over the memory of her at eighteen, wearing that look when he'd tried to ask her to prom.

These past thirty-six hours had brought her back into his life and shown him the kind of woman she really was. The kind of woman who mourned for the daughter she never got to have. The woman who was patient enough to listen to Lily's convoluted stories over breakfast. The artist. Her voice from the cassette had faded, but was forever held in his memory. She was amazingly talented. Also amazingly beautiful and kind.

But she wasn't staying in Redbud Trails. When she went back to her life in Nashville, she'd forget all about him.

And if he wanted to keep from getting eviscerated, he couldn't kiss her again.

So he settled for pressing his chin against her temple and holding her loosely.

"You'll find your voice again," he whispered into her hair.

And then he squeezed her elbows and let her go.

CHAPTER 6

*S*tevie had gone upstairs as Jake closed up the downstairs.

She ducked into the bathroom first. She didn't like the disconnect between them. Jake felt...distant. She hadn't wanted it, but Zack's appearance had changed everything. Reality had intruded on her interlude.

When she'd finished washing her face, she crossed the hall to the guest room.

An acoustic guitar rested across the corner of the bed. And a sticky note was propped next to it.

It's Courtney's. Thought you might want to borrow it. Jake's masculine scrawl was distinctive, and she imagined it across his students' papers.

She sat on the bed, almost afraid to touch the instrument.

She stared at it for a long time, barely breathing.

She reached out and tweaked one string. It sounded horrible. Out of tune.

She ran the tip of her finger over the curved body. It was cool and smooth to the touch.

What had Jake been thinking when he'd brought this in and left it? She'd *just* told him that she couldn't write. Had he meant it as a challenge?

He'd offered her such comfort over the last days, she couldn't imagine that he'd brought it in here to hurt her.

She picked it up. Pain arced through her chest.

Breathing through her mouth, she tried to fight through it. She didn't have to play anything. Didn't have to feel the music, feel the pain.

She could tune it, though.

Her fingers fumbled with the tuning key. She gritted her teeth as the first rough chord emanated from the guitar.

First string. Second string. Sixth string.

The fingers of her right hand played along the strings without plucking any of them.

She pulled one note. It sounded clear and pure in the empty room.

And her heart broke all over again.

After several moments, she scrambled off the bed and grabbed her duffel bag off the floor. She'd gotten in the habit of never leaving home without a blank notepad and pencil, and she dug for them, finally coming up with both.

She settled back on the bed, her back against the pillows and headboard, the guitar across her lap.

She let her fingers play over the strings, not truly picking out notes that went together. She turned her face up to the ceiling as tears streamed from the sides of her eyes and down below her ears.

As she let the music stream through her, she allowed her silent pictures of Sienna to run through her in slow motion, along with the music notes.

And then she started writing. Softly, aware that Lily slept just down the hall.

IT HAD BEEN A GAMBLE, putting Courtney's old guitar in Stevie's room. Like skipping the approximations and trying the full set of equations first.

But it seemed to have paid off.

Jake sat in the dark hallway, his back to the wall. Stevie's music flowed through the crack beneath the door. The notes began melancholy and slow. Then changed to fast and almost angry. That lasted for awhile.

And then, finally, the music changed to something soft and almost haunting.

At one point, she replayed the same series of notes over and over. Slowly, and then with pauses in between the different parts, as if she was writing it down.

He sat listening, heart pounding as hard as it had been earlier. Empty.

She was doing it. She was facing her demons, facing down the grief.

And she was winning.

Her healing wouldn't be linear. He knew there would likely be days—often surprising her—where the grief would hit her and maybe even knock her down.

But she was taking the first steps to memorialize Sienna.

And that meant that she wouldn't need him anymore.

IN THE MORNING, Jake woke to a soft knock at his bedroom door. He forced his sand-filled eyes open—he'd listened to Stevie playing guitar until the wee hours of the morning.

It was still dark outside.

He forced his feet to the floor and stumbled to the door. Stevie stood in the hallway, her hair rumpled but still wearing the same clothes from last night.

She appeared tired, but her face was alight.

"I know it's a lot to ask," she whispered. "But I need to go to Nashville today—and I wondered if you'd go with me. I want to visit Sienna's grave."

"Of course I will."

CHAPTER 7

*S*tevie woke to Jake shaking her shoulder. "We're here."

She opened her eyes to find his face only inches away.

She blinked at him, for a startling second not remembering the last twenty-four hours, only remembering the power of his kiss.

And then he broke eye contact, shutting his emotions off from her and sitting back in his seat.

She straightened and pushed off from the passenger door, and everything came back to her. Her marathon sleepless night writing Sienna's song. Asking Jake to come with her.

He'd scrambled for a babysitter early in the morning and then, when his friend's wife had shown up, he'd loaded Stevie into her car, and they'd taken off for Nashville. He'd used his phone to book a plane ticket back to Oklahoma and would fly back late in the day.

And he'd come with her. He'd been the truest friend she'd had since she'd left Redbud Trails at nineteen.

He had to feel the connection between them. It wasn't something she planned to let go, even back on tour. She'd let her life get out of whack, been solely focused on her career. And that wasn't healthy. She was determined to do things right this time around—Sienna's passing had taught her that.

She needed down time. Needed time for the things in life that were more important. Like a life.

She ran one hand through her hair. She probably looked like the wicked witch of the west after sleeping for several hours in the car.

She looked at the black wrought iron fence that surrounded the cemetery just outside the passenger window.

She took a deep breath. She didn't know if she could do this. But then, she hadn't thought she'd be able to write music again either.

Jake rested his hand over hers on her thigh. He seemed to know what she needed without her asking. He didn't try to help with meaningless platitudes. He just sat with her. Listened to her.

She took a deep breath and opened the door.

Jake had been kind enough to loan her his sister's guitar, so she didn't have to stop at her apartment, and she took it out of the backseat, removing it from its black leather case.

As they approached the grass beyond the sidewalk,

her stomach dropped, and all the blood in her head whooshed to her feet.

Jake's hand on her lower back steadied her.

Everything was damp from an early afternoon rain. It was noticeably different here than in Oklahoma. The trees were taller. The air felt heavier, cooler.

They found Sienna's grave in a row of others. The dirt above where her casket was buried was fresh and bulged above the ground.

And that broke the dam of her tears again.

Jake offered her a handkerchief—so old fashioned—and stood beside her silently as she wept all over again.

When she'd calmed as much as she was going to, she sat cross-legged on the grass beside Sienna's headstone.

And she began to play.

She would never play this song in public. It was Sienna's song. A song of a life cut too short, of the girl who'd been bright and funny and shouldn't have gone so soon.

JAKE SAT across from Stevie in what she'd said was her favorite coffee shop in a trendy part of Nashville.

She'd played and mourned over Sienna's grave for more than an hour.

There was no danger of missing his flight, so they'd stopped for coffee when she'd suggested it would be a great way to warm up and dry off.

The coffee house was miles different from the drive-thru Coffee Hut back home. A long line of customers snaked through the trendy, tiny tables.

He'd angled his chair carefully so their knees wouldn't bump.

She played with the straw in her cup. "I never thought when I drove up your driveway that I'd come out of this with a new best friend."

Friends again. Was she giving him the friends speech preventatively? Before he could make a fool of himself all over again? His gut clenched in a tight little ball. As if he'd be that stupid twice in the same lifetime.

"You and Lily have some major adjustments on the horizon. I hope you'll lean on me when the time comes."

That's what he needed to do, focus on Lily and everything waiting on him back home. Getting ready for Courtney's release in a few months. Christmas was coming up.

She tilted her head to one side, planted her elbow on the table, and leaned her cheek on one fist. She looked almost...expectant. What did she want him to say? That he'd call her every day?

She was going back to her regular life, one that would soon be too busy for the likes of him.

Before he could think of anything to say, a bright light flashed across the room. He didn't think anything of it, but Stevie's attention focused on it, and her expression closed down.

"We need to go," she said in a low voice. She stood, banging her leg against the table's edge.

He followed her lead, noticing that the din of voices had grown louder. He reached for the trash on their table, but she clutched his elbow. "Leave it."

He noted the urgency in her voice and the squeeze of her hand.

He turned, and that's when he noticed multiple cameramen crowding inside near the doorway. Their cameras were pointed at Stevie.

Something protective rose up in him, and he put himself in front of her.

She grabbed the back of his shirt and followed him toward the door.

"Excuse me," he said to the first of the paparazzi when he got near.

They didn't move.

"Stevie, who's your new flame?"

"What's your name?"

They shouted questions at the both of them.

"Don't talk to them," Stevie whispered into his ear. She must've been standing on her tiptoes to get close enough that her breath warmed his neck.

If they weren't going to move, he was going to have to push his way through. He put his elbow into the first guy, who didn't so much move as shift.

They were jostled, and he tucked Stevie beneath his arm and tried to guide her past.

They reached the door, and he pushed it open so she could go through.

For a second, he gazed down at her.

And then they were outside on the empty sidewalk. Paparazzi streamed out after them, still shouting questions.

He looked to Stevie.

"Run."

He grabbed her hand, and they took off toward her car.

Stevie had apologized profusely, but Jake shrugged off what had happened at the coffeeshop as she'd navigated the traffic toward the airport.

She could guess—although she wouldn't be able to confirm it until later—who'd clued the press in on her location.

As soon as she dropped Jake off at the airport, she was firing Zack. And deleting all the apps from her phone.

It was time for a change.

The airport traffic was only moderately busy, and she found a spot at the curb near his departure gate. Cars zoomed by in the passing lanes. People on the sidewalk wheeled or carried their luggage, both coming and going.

She got out and met him at the curb as he exited the car. He slung the backpack that he'd come with over his shoulder and gripped the guitar case in his other hand.

"Thank you for coming with me," she said.

She couldn't read his expression. He seemed distant again. Like she couldn't reach him. It made her suddenly shy.

"Thank you for everything," she whispered.

He nodded. A muscle jumped in his cheek.

Tears stung behind her nose. She wasn't ready to part from him, not really, but she had obligations.

She had to start getting her career on the track she wanted. It was going to take time.

"Can I call you?" she asked. "And Lily?"

He hesitated. Nodded slowly. The roar of a plane nearby muted the beginning of his answer. "...too busy."

"I'm not going to be too busy," she said firmly.

But the resigned look in his eyes said he thought differently.

A security guy started toward them, and she knew they weren't going to let her car stay at the curb for much longer.

"Be careful," she whispered.

She reached for him, and he put one arm around her in a side-hug.

It wasn't the embrace he'd offered her yesterday, or the comfort he'd given her earlier at the cemetery. But how could she ask for more when he'd given her so much already?

She let him go.

He strode toward the glass doors, nodding to the security guard as he approached and then passed the man.

Her heart thudded a refrain. *Wrong. Wrong. Wrong.*

How could she let him walk away like this when she'd promised herself she was going to take every chance when it came.

She couldn't.

"Wait! Jake!"

She rushed toward him, as he stopped and turned toward her.

"I promise I'll move my car in just a second," she said to the security guy as she brushed past him.

Jake's surprise was evident in his eyes, but he met her, and his arms came around her again, both of them this time. The guitar case banged against the back of her legs.

She rose on her tiptoes, wrapped her arms around his neck, and kissed him.

His mouth was warm and firm, and she tried to pour everything she felt for him into the kiss. Her gratitude. Her admiration.

Her love.

She loved him.

It was the worst time to realize it, when he was getting ready to get on a plane.

She couldn't say it. She pulled back slightly, enough to look up into his dear face.

He gazed down at her, and she almost thought she saw her feelings reflected back at her, but still the words stuck in her throat.

But her heart played a melody she would never forget. Jake's song.

"Bye," she whispered.

"Bye," he said.

He brushed one more kiss across her forehead, and then he let her go.

She watched him walk into the terminal without looking back.

CHAPTER 8

*J*ake got the email from his mom three days after he'd flown back to Oklahoma. It was a screenshot from a tabloid website. He slumped back in his office chair as he looked it over.

At the bottom right-hand corner, there was a high-resolution shot of him and Stevie as they'd pushed out of that Nashville coffeeshop.

Country star Stevie Flower with new boyfriend? the headline read.

But it wasn't the headline or the text that had his mouth going dry and his palms going moist.

It was the way the photographer had captured the photo. It showed every nuance of Jake's face as he'd looked down on her for that brief second.

Everything he felt for her was written across his face for the world to see.

He loved her.

The phone on his desk rang. It had to be his mom.

It was.

He braced himself, expecting criticism or gloating that she'd been right, but what she asked was, "Are you okay?"

"I'm fine, Mom. Lily and I are settling back into our routine after the break. She's excited to go trick-or-treating this weekend. Everything's normal." Except for the gaping wormhole in his midsection.

"So you don't...want to talk about it?"

He took of his glasses and closed his eyes, pinching the bridge of his nose between his thumb and forefinger. "Talk about what?"

"You had a thing for that girl back in high school, but I didn't realize you *loved* her."

He really didn't want to discuss this. "Nobody was supposed to find out. Not her. Not you."

"Well, then you shouldn't have had your picture taken for the whole world to see."

He pressed his fist into his forehead. "She's gone back to her life, and Lily and I have gone back to ours. Everything's fine."

He doubted his mom bought the lie, but she ended the call with, "I'm sorry, baby."

He let the receiver crash into its cradle.

He'd thought his feelings from high school were adolescent and long-gone, but with her presence in his house, with the way she'd been with Lily, all those feelings had come rushing back.

Stronger.

But he didn't intend to *act* on them. Not after what'd

happened in high school, and not when it was clear they didn't belong in each other's dimensions. He'd never intended for her to know how he felt.

But if she saw this photo, she'd know.

Maybe she wouldn't see it. Or maybe she would call him, like she'd asked to do when they'd parted in Nashville. And maybe he'd hear in her voice a tone that matched the expression he never wanted to see again.

Please God, don't let her call to let him down with the *friends* speech.

He'd never prayed so hard for anything in his life.

TWO WEEKS LATER, Jake walked down the hallway in the on-campus science building toward his office. He'd forced himself to go eat with a group of the other professors instead of holing up in his office.

He greeted a couple of students who had been in last semester's physics lab. Other voices echoed down the cinderblock hallway, kids on their way to or from class.

Someone was waiting near his door. Which wasn't unusual. He often had students who wanted to talk about assignments or extra credit or test grades.

But when he realized who it was, he stopped dead in his tracks.

It was Stevie. Stevie was waiting for him.

He found his feet again and started toward her. She looked good. She was wearing a slim denim skirt, cowboy boots, and a flowing peasant shirt. She had a tote bag over her shoulder.

"Hey."

"Hey." What a great line. He was such a loser. He hadn't heard from her since they'd parted at the airport in Nashville, but he'd thought about her daily. Hourly.

He'd figured she'd probably seen the tabloid picture and decided it wasn't worth the awkwardness to keep their friendship.

Her eyes took him in from head to toe, and he realized what she was seeing. It had been lab day for his Chem I class, so he wore his lab coat on over his slacks and polo shirt. He reached up and touched his hair, trying to smooth down what he knew he'd inadvertently mussed while grading papers in his office earlier.

He must look like the mad scientist. How much more geeky could he get?

His chest banded tight, but he didn't shuck his jacket when he went into the office and motioned her in. This was who he was.

It's who he'd been in high school and it's who he was now, and there was no sense pretending he could be anything different, even for her.

"What brings you out here?" Campus wasn't exactly on any route to any big city.

She rummaged in her tote and came up with a newspaper.

His heart sank even as his pulse thundered in his ears.

She flipped the folded paper toward him, even though he already knew what she was going to show him.

The photo.

"I've seen it." He was amazed at how calm his voice sounded.

"I found out Zack sicced the paparazzi on us. I'm sorry about that."

He shrugged. "Only ten or twelve of the ladies at church gave me a hard time about it." Not including his mom.

This was all right. He could act like it didn't matter. Maybe she didn't see what he'd thought was so obvious.

His chest went tight again. He remembered that moment in the orchard when she'd told him not to be intimidated anymore.

And the kiss she'd given him at the airport.

About Adam, who always said he should *go big*.

He went around his desk, maybe putting distance between them on purpose.

But now she moved closer. "Can I ask you a question about this picture?"

The minute amount of tension that had bled out of him returned in full force. "What about it?" he asked warily.

She put the tabloid on the corner of the desk and placed her index finger just above his head on the photo. "The photographer who took the photo...they made it look like you were in love with me."

There was an expectant pause. His brain wailed a warning, the memory of her *rescue-me* face. But he took a deep breath. He didn't have Stevie now, and when she rejected him, nothing would have changed. He'd already made himself the fool for her once, practically scared himself away from girls forever. What did he have to lose?

"That's because I am," he said, and then added, just in case, "in love with you."

It was difficult to meet her eyes, but he did it. He wanted to see hope there, but maybe he'd misread the whole situation. Again. "I have been since high school." The words just continued to fall from his lips.

He thought he heard a soft indrawn breath pass through her lips, but then she looked down at where her finger still touched the paper. Her hair fell into her face, so he couldn't read her reaction. Not that he'd be able to, even if he could see.

She nodded slowly. "Well, then."

What did *well, then* mean?

She half-turned, and his heart hammered. Had she come all this way just to confront him about the picture and leave? She approached the door, and something screamed in his mind to memorize the sight. The last time he'd ever see her in person.

But she didn't walk out.

She dug in her tote and came up with a stack of thick, white papers.

Then she began unfolding it, and he realized it wasn't papers at all, but a poster board that had been folded into fourths. As she unfolded it to its full size, he saw loopy, glittery words. *"Will you go to prom with me?"*

His face burned. "I wasn't sure you remembered that." She certainly hadn't brought it up while they'd been together.

But if *she* were holding the sign up for *him*...? Was she asking him out? No, surely not. Something else?

"I was immature back then. Too stupid and worried about what my friends thought to realize what we could be together."

She took a breath, and he noticed her hands were shaking. The poster board was shimmering in her grip.

"Then I let my career take over my life," she continued. "And it took Sienna"—her voice trembled—"and you to show me that I needed to get my life back."

He couldn't stand the distance between them anymore. He circled the desk and took the poster from her hands. He set it on his desk, then pulled her close. She came into his arms easily, as if she belonged there.

He cleared emotion from his throat. "It's sort of too late for prom, but I'll go out with you tonight, as long as I don't have to rent a tux."

Against his shoulder, he felt her nod.

"I love you too, you know," she said.

His breath, and the last of his tension, left him in a rush. "I didn't know. I never expected..."

She loved him. Joy swirled in crazy spirals through him. He bent his head, and she met him in a sweet kiss that quickly deepened to something more.

He put a minuscule amount of distance between them, pressing his lips to her forehead briefly instead.

She sighed softly. "I don't know exactly how this is going to work. I haven't had a successful relationship since I got into the music industry."

He squeezed her waist gently.

"But then, I've never felt this way about anyone before."

When she said stuff like that, he felt about like Superman. As if he could fly and lift skyscrapers. Invincible.

"We'll make it work," he said.

"I've scaled back my tour dates for next year. I can't do anything about the contracts we've already signed for this year. And I'm sure I can find a studio in Oklahoma City when I'm ready to record."

"I can renovate the barn again," he offered. "Build you a studio here."

She laughed softly. "We'll see."

"Depending on how things are going with Lily after Courtney gets out next spring, maybe I can go on tour with you for part of the summer."

"Mmm. That sounds nice." She instigated the kiss this time, only she placed small, gentle kisses against the corners of his lips. "Especially if we're married by then."

Married?

She laughed at what must be the dumbfounded expression on his face. "You do want to get married, right?" Her eyebrows lifted. "Eventually...?"

He nodded dumbly. "Yes, please."

Her eyes fell closed, her lashes lowering to hide her eyes from him. "I wrote a song for you," she whispered.

"I hope it's a romantic one."

"It is. I'm thinking of putting it on my next album."

"I'm okay with that. Then everyone will know you're mine."

Because she was.

*C*ameras flashed on the steps of the Oklahoma City courthouse.

This time, Stevie had been the one to notify the press. She wanted her actions today recorded for posterity.

She gazed up at Jake, and his chin dipped in a grin that only gave a hint at his true feelings. Tiny snowflakes dotted his hair and eyelashes.

It was cold, and she was starting to shiver, so they wouldn't be staying long.

Downtown Oklahoma City was ready for Christmas. Many businesses had decorated with lights and pine boughs. Evergreen wreaths strung with red ribbons hung from streetlights, and the sound of Christmas carols drifted from the manmade ice rink down the street.

Jake looked incredibly handsome in a black button-down shirt, black jeans, and boots. A black dress Stetson rounded out the outfit. He looked nothing like the professor, but he'd confided to her earlier that he wore one of his science T-shirts beneath. She was proud of his profession, even if she only understood it when he explained slowly and with much repetition. It was a part of who he was.

Her knee-length lace dress and brown cowgirl boots weren't doing much to keep her warm, even with the ivory coat she wore over her ensemble.

The diamond on the fourth finger of her left hand caught the light just right from where she posed with her hands on Jake's shoulders, one foot kicked up behind her. The plain gold band didn't have as much shine, but almost meant more.

They'd opted for a short ceremony in front of a county judge. Mostly for expediency. Stevie's tour would start up with a vengeance again in January, and Jake's break would be up soon after the new year. They wanted to cram as much time together as they could before they were pulled in different directions.

Lily had witnessed the ceremony with them inside, but Jake's friends had taken her out the back of the building. Jake didn't mind some minor time in the media's spotlight, but neither of them wanted Lily exposed. Especially with Courtney's release date set for early next summer, the less drama for all involved the better. Stevie had gone to visit Courtney a couple times, once with her new publicist, and they'd talked over some strategies to keep Lily out of the limelight.

The media interest in Stevie had died down to almost nothing after she'd fired Zack. Turned out the jerk had been making up stories and circulating them, along with the occasional true tip about her whereabouts or inside details.

She'd hired a great attorney, and they'd placed a gag order on her former manager. Her new manager, Lorraine, had told a few people in the right places in the industry about the things Zack had done, and word had it Zack was having trouble getting new clients.

"Lorraine is giving me the two minute signal," Jake murmured in her ear, holding her even closer for some shots.

"About time," she returned, turning her face up to his for a kiss. His lips were cool, but the kiss warmed her from the inside out.

Stevie was insanely happy, but there was still an empty place inside that ached. Sienna's chunk of her heart.

"Ready?" Lorraine approached and handed them the white balloons filled with helium. The winter wind tried to tug them away. The manager backed down the steps again.

This would be the last photo op, and then Lorraine would shoo away the reporters.

Jake's hand closed over hers on the ribbons. They both craned their heads back, looking at the bobbing balloons. Maybe Jake was as lost in memories and wishes as she was.

One balloon each for the people who should've been here with them. Adam and Sienna.

Jake squeezed her hand, and they both let go and watched the balloons fly up into the sky. Past the nearest building. Past the skyscrapers until they disappeared in the snow-filled clouds.

She still missed Sienna. She always would.

But God had given her this chance with Jake and Lily, and she wasn't going to take it for granted. They'd wrangle schedules and tour dates and recording contracts, and they'd do it together.

And maybe eventually, they'd name their first daughter Sienna.

They were a family now. And there was no going back.

The Lost Princess

Made in the USA
Coppell, TX
22 October 2021

64448830R10059